THE PHANTOM LOLLIPOP MAN!

PAMELA
BUTCHART

nosy
crow

Look out for:

BABY ALIENS GOT MY TEACHER!

THE SPY WHO LOVED SCHOOL DINNERS

MY HEADTEACHER IS A VAMPIRE RAT!

ATTACK OF THE DEMON DINNER LADIES

TO WEE OR NOT TO WEE!

THERE'S A WEREWOLF IN MY TENT!

THERE'S A YETI IN THE PLAYGROUND!

ICARUS WAS RIDICULOUS

THE BROKEN LEG OF DOOM

For
Slugathor
x x x

First published in the UK in 2018 by Nosy Crow Ltd
The Crow's Nest, 14 Baden Place, Crosby Row,
London, SE1 1YW, UK

Nosy Crow and associated logos are trademarks and/or registered
trademarks of Nosy Crow Ltd.

Text copyright © Pamela Butchart, 2018
Cover and illustrations copyright © Thomas Flintham, 2018

ISBN: 978 1 78800 048 2

A CIP catalogue record for this book will be available from the British Library.

Printed and bound in Great Britain by Clays Ltd, Elcograf S.p.A.

Papers used by Nosy Crow are made from wood grown in sustainable forests.

MIX
Paper from
responsible sources
FSC® C018072
www.fsc.org

9

www.nosycrow.com

Contents

Something Seriously Spooky

One time something SERIOUSLY SPOOKY happened at our school and even though Jodi (that's my best friend) wants to be an actual GHOST FINDER when she's older, even SHE wasn't FULLY PREPARED.

It all started when the LOLLIPOP man went MISSING.

Our friend Maisie said that the LOLLIPOP man might have gone on holiday to ROME.

But then when we spoke to the OFFICE LADIES we found out that the LOLLIPOP man definitely HADN'T gone to Rome!

And that's when everything got really

SPOOKY

with the NEBULOUS CLOUD and KARLY-WITH-A-K and the FIRE ALARM and the BLACKOUT!

Our other best friend, Zach, said we probably should have been wearing

GHOST PROTECTION SUITS

from **DAY ONE** and that if we had, I probably wouldn't have ended up with **HOLEY TIGHTS!**

Jodi said that we all had to become **GHOST AWARE** asap.

Especially when we saw the

FLOATING LOLLIPOP STICK!

And most people have never been to an actual **GHOST PARTY** in their lives.

But we have.

4

Bad
News

When we arrived at school on Monday, Maisie said, "Who's THAT?" And then she pointed to the LOLLIPOP man.

That's when I saw that it wasn't our normal LOLLIPOP man and that it was actually a LOLLIPOP LADY.

So we all went over and Jodi said, "Who are you, please?" And I knew that she said "please" because of one time when we went to the takeaway around the corner from Jodi's house and there was a new person serving the food and Jodi said, "Who are you?" and the new person said, "None of your business! Who are YOU?" And then Jodi's mum made us wait outside while she

"HAD WORDS"

with the new person and then she didn't have to pay for the chips that day and she told Jodi that she should always say please when she asks who someone is.

So anyway, the **LOLLIPOP** lady smiled at us and said, "I'm Mabel. Pleased to meet you."

And we all just looked at each other because the old **LOLLIPOP** man **NEVER** smiled at us and I don't think he was really pleased about meeting any of us.

So we asked Mabel if she knew what had happened to the old LOLLIPOP man but she said that she didn't and that she was sorry and we said that was OK because it wasn't her fault she didn't know.

Jodi said that maybe the LOLLIPOP man was off sick or something and I thought that she was probably right because the LOLLIPOP man was REALLY old and I was sure that he must've been almost one hundred years old. Maisie said that she hoped the LOLLIPOP man was OK because even though most people do not like the LOLLIPOP man because he's

REALLY GRUMPY

and he shouts at us and waves his **LOLLIPOP** stick about if he doesn't like the way we're crossing the road, he seems to like Maisie and he even speaks to her a bit and asks us where she is when she's not with us.

So I said that he had probably just gone away for a long weekend like my gran does when she goes to Blackpool and Maisie smiled and said she thought I was right and that she hoped he had gone to Rome.

But the **LOLLIPOP** man wasn't back the

next day. Or the day after that. And when we arrived at school on Friday and the LOLLIPOP man STILL wasn't back Maisie said that she thought something had

GONE WRONG

in Rome and that she could feel it in her BONES and that maybe the LOLLIPOP man had been

KIDNAPPED.

Jodi looked at me and I looked at Jodi

because we were both thinking the same thing. And that was that the LOLLIPOP man HADN'T been kidnapped in Rome and that he had probably been SACKED and REPLACED by the new, younger LOLLIPOP lady who actually SMILED at people and seemed not to hate everyone like the old LOLLIPOP man did.

But before we could say anything Zach said, "I'll ask Miss Jones," and he got up and wandered over to Miss Jones's desk.

Maisie STARED at Miss Jones when

Zach spoke to her and so did we because Miss Jones had a

WEIRD LOOK

on her face and then she went a bit RED like the time she accidentally said a SWEAR when she couldn't fit the school minibus into any of the parking spaces at Tesco when Gary Petrie needed a wee and people kept tooting their car horns at us.

When Zach got back from Miss Jones's desk he said that she didn't know if the LOLLIPOP man was sick or not and that

Miss Jones had seemed really

CONFUSED

when he asked her and that it seemed like she didn't actually **KNOW** who he was talking about.

We all thought it was a bit **WEIRD** that Miss Jones didn't know who the **LOLLIPOP** man was because he'd been here since we were in Year One and maybe even before that.

But Jodi said that Miss Jones probably never needed his help to cross the road

13

because she always gets here really early and parks her car right outside the classroom. Then Jodi said she wasn't sure grown-ups were even **ALLOWED** to use the **LOLLIPOP** man and that **LOLLIPOP** people were probably only allowed to help people who were under sixteen cross the road and that they probably even asked to see their passports as **PROOF OF AGE**.

That's when Maisie said we needed to ask

EVERY SINGLE PERSON IN THE SCHOOL

why the LOLLIPOP man was missing and what hospital they thought he might have been taken to so that we could all go and visit at the weekend and take him some Lucozade and grapes.

So at break we wandered around the playground asking people about the LOLLIPOP man. But nobody knew where he was. Then Jodi said, "That's it. We're going to have to ask the OFFICE LADIES. They'll definitely know."

Maisie

Even though Jodi was very right to say that the office ladies would know (because the office ladies know EVERYTHING!) it was still a bit of a dangerous thing to do because:

1. The office ladies are SERIOUSLY SCARY!
2. They make you wait at the glass window for AGES while they pretend that they can't see you.
3. The office ladies HATE being asked any questions (even though answering questions is their job).

When we got to the school office, Jodi said that she wasn't going to be the one to go up to the glass window because she had

17

been the one who came up with the idea to ask the office ladies and that it was someone else's turn.

So I just looked down at the ground and didn't say anything because I was hoping Zach would say he would go because usually we just make him do it anyway.

But then nobody said anything for ages and when I looked up I saw that Zach was looking down at the ground, too. And also that Maisie was covering her face with her hair.

So that's when I said, "Fine. I'll go," and I took a deep breath and walked over to the glass window and knocked on the wall beneath it because the window is too high up to reach. And my granddad says that that's what the office ladies DEMANDED when the school was first being built and he knows that for a FACT because he helped build my school ages ago when he came back from The War.

So anyway, the glass window slid open but before I could even say ONE WORD it SLAMMED SHUT again.

I looked over at Jodi and she did her WIDE

EYES at me so I took another deep breath
and knocked on the wall again.

When the glass door opened, I shouted,

"I'M DOWN HERE!"

before it could shut again. That's when one of the office ladies stuck her head out and I saw RIGHT up her nose.

My hands were

SWEATING

but I just wiped them on my skirt and said, "I'm really sorry but I need to ask you a question." The office lady sighed REALLY loudly and then muttered something to one of the other office ladies inside the office and then THEY sighed, too. The office lady didn't say anything after the sigh, but she didn't close the glass door either, so that's when I said, "Where's the old LOLLIPOP man gone, please?"

The office lady leaned out of the window further and I could see that she had a long, dark hair under her chin which was a bit weird because she was a lady and also because it was just one long hair and I wasn't sure how it got there or why she didn't just pull it out.

Then she said, "Who?!"

So I said, "There's a new LOLLIPOP man that's a lady. What happened to the old LOLLIPOP man?"

The office lady slid the glass door shut and

started whispering to the other office ladies inside. So I put my ear against the wall to try to hear what they were whispering about but I couldn't.

Then the other office lady stuck her head RIGHT out of the window and said, "The LOLLIPOP man has moved on."

And then she slammed the little door shut. And that's when I heard

SCREAMING.

Who's Jack??

Once the nurse EVENTUALLY let us in to see Maisie, I thought Maisie was going to tell us that she'd screamed and fainted into the big pot plant because she'd heard that the LOLLIPOP man had MOVED ON.

But when we sat on the end of the little

bed in the nurse's office, Maisie said that she had gotten the

FRIGHT OF HER LIFE

when the office lady leaned out of the window because she thought the office lady had been trying to "get" me.

I looked at Zach and Zach looked at Jodi because we knew that if Maisie HADN'T heard what the office ladies had said about the LOLLIPOP man MOVING ON, she didn't realise that they obviously meant that the LOLLIPOP man had PASSED AWAY.

Then Jodi said, "Maisie, why don't you have a little rest and I'll make sure Miss Jones knows where you are. We'll come back and get you at lunchtime, OK?"

Maisie nodded and Jodi gave us a LOOK

and we knew that it meant that we shouldn't tell Maisie about the LOLLIPOP man just now because she was already in a bit of a state about the scary office lady.

Jodi went off to speak to the school nurse while me and Zach tucked Maisie in and poured her a juice.

When we got outside Jodi said that she'd told the nurse that she should

UNDER NO
CIRCUMSTANCES

tell Maisie about the LOLLIPOP man passing away. And that the nurse hadn't known about the LOLLIPOP man passing away. But when we went back to the nurse's office at lunchtime, the nurse wasn't there and neither was Maisie.

So we went to the dinner hall to see if she was there. But she wasn't. And she wasn't in the toilets either.

That's when me and Zach started to PANIC but Jodi said,

"STOP!"

because Jodi is very good at calming everyone down when they start freaking out. Like the time we went to the museum and Jodi had to grab our old head teacher, Mr Murphy, by the arms and give him a bit of a shake because he started crying and screaming a bit when he couldn't find Nola Burke, even though Nola Burke hadn't even been on the trip that day because she'd had chicken pox.

So anyway, that's when Jodi said, "We need to get INSIDE MAISIE'S HEAD. Think, people! Where would Maisie go if she was scared?"

And that's when we knew where she'd be.

We all RAN to The Den (which is our secret

room under the stairs that go up to the boys'
toilets that no one except us knows about).
But Maisie wasn't there.

Then Zach said that Maisie had probably
seen the office lady again and started
HYPERVENTILATING and been taken
away by ambulance with an OXYGEN
MASK on, like the time she found the

DEAD MOUSE.

But then all of a sudden we heard the SECRET KNOCK on The Den door, so Jodi did the secret knock back and then moved the chair away and opened the door and it was Maisie and she had a big smile on her face.

We thought that she might be in SHOCK.

And we knew that for a FACT when we asked Maisie where she had been because she said, "I went to say hello to Jack but by the time I got outside, he'd disappeared!"

Zach asked Maisie if Jack was one of the PARAMEDICS who had helped her with the OXYGEN MASK.

But Maisie shook her head and said, "Jack the LOLLIPOP man.

He's BACK!"

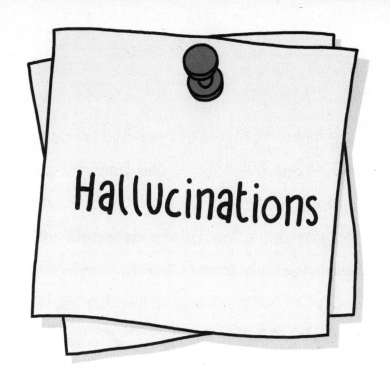

Hallucinations

Jodi gasped and covered her mouth with both hands.

We all looked at each other but we had **NO IDEA** what to say because Maisie had clearly hit her head when she fainted into the big pot plant.

I gently took Maisie's hands and made her sit down on the floor of The Den and Jodi put the chair back against the door. And then she put a few boxes there too and I knew she did it so that Maisie couldn't run away when we explained to her that she was

SEEING THINGS.

Zach said that he was going to make Maisie a nice cup of tea (even though we don't have a kettle and we just use cold water from the little sink and a tea bag, so it's not really that nice actually).

The WHOLE TIME Zach was making the tea Maisie kept talking about how happy she'd been when she spotted Jack through the window in the nurse's office.

I just smiled and nodded as Maisie chatted away because I didn't know what else to do because she was obviously still having

HALLUCINATIONS.

That's when Maisie noticed that we were all behaving a bit strangely and also that Jodi was inspecting her head for LUMPS. Maisie asked us what was going on but Jodi just said, "NOTHING!" and then she began tidying up The Den and whistling loads.

But Maisie KNEW that we were HIDING SOMETHING from her and she started to PANIC that it was something SCARY like when we had

DEMON DINNER LADIES

at our school.

So that's when Zach told her about the LOLLIPOP man moving on.

But Maisie just shook her head and said, "You're WRONG. I just saw him!"

So Jodi stroked Maisie's hair and said, "No, Maisie. You just THINK you saw him. You imagined it because you were in SHOCK after hitting your head on the pot plant."

That's when Maisie said, "I DIDN'T imagine it! I saw him!"

But Jodi said it didn't really make sense because the school wouldn't have needed the NEW LOLLIPOP lady if the LOLLIPOP man hadn't MOVED ON.

But Maisie stood up and said that we were COMPLETELY WRONG and that she had DEFINITELY seen him and that she was feeling FINE and that she was not SEEING THINGS because of the pot plant. So I explained that it had been the OFFICE LADY who had told us and that's when Maisie

GASPED.

She shook her head backwards and forwards for ages because she knew that the office ladies know **EVERYTHING** and that they are

ALWAYS RIGHT.

But then Zach said, "Erm ... there might actually be a way that **BOTH** things are true. The **LOLLIPOP** man **COULD** have moved on **AND** Maisie could have just seen him."

Then Zach looked at me for AGES and I just KNEW what he was going to say before he said it and why he was looking specifically at ME.

And that was because Zach knew he was about to say my

MOST SCARIEST THING EVER.

And he did.

Zach said, "I think the LOLLIPOP man might be a

PHANTOM!"

Phantom!

Usually everyone is trying to calm MAISIE down because she's pretty much scared of EVERYTHING and one time she actually called 999 because someone sneezed on her arm.

But this time everyone was trying to calm

ME down because I was shaking my arms **ALL OVER THE PLACE** and I could hear

but I didn't realise until afterwards that it had been coming from me.

Jodi put the palm of her hand against my head and said, "**SLEEP!**" because she'd

seen that magician on TV do it to people when he hypnotises them and then does things like tell them everyone in the world is a ZOMBIE now and then they start freaking out.

But it didn't work.

Then I heard Zach say that someone was going to have to SLAP me across the face to

SNAP ME OUT OF IT

and then Jodi started counting down from five so I calmed down. Maisie sat next to me and showed me how to do the SPECIAL BREATHING TECHNIQUE that her doctor had shown her for when she has a PANIC ATTACK. And that worked a bit.

But then Jodi said that we had to go looking for the phantom **LOLLIPOP** man to make sure we were right and that's the last thing I remember.

When I woke up I felt

REALLY WARM

and I could hear whispering and the squeaky sound the Official Secret Meeting Pen makes on the little whiteboard that Jodi accidently stole.

I sat up and realised that Maisie, Zach and

Jodi were having a meeting about

THE PHANTOM
LOLLIPOP MAN

and also that I couldn't move my arms or my legs!

But then Maisie noticed that I was awake and she smiled and crawled over and started taking off all the blankets that were wrapped around me and I realised that I must have

fainted and that Maisie had wrapped me up
tight and let me have a little nap just like we
do when she faints.

It was

REALLY WEIRD

being the one who had fainted and missing
a bit of the secret meeting and I realised that
that's what Maisie must feel like all the time.
Zach gave me a Twix and Jodi told me to
eat it all for STRENGTH so that she could
update me on the CURRENT SITUATION.
So I did.

That's when Jodi said that they'd been
researching PHANTOMS on Zach's phone.

I looked at Maisie. She didn't look scared

at ALL (which was

MEGA WEIRD

because she'd just seen

a **PHANTOM!**).

Zach said that they'd managed to find out LOADS and that Jodi had even known TONNES OF STUFF before they started researching.

Then Jodi turned the whiteboard around and it said:

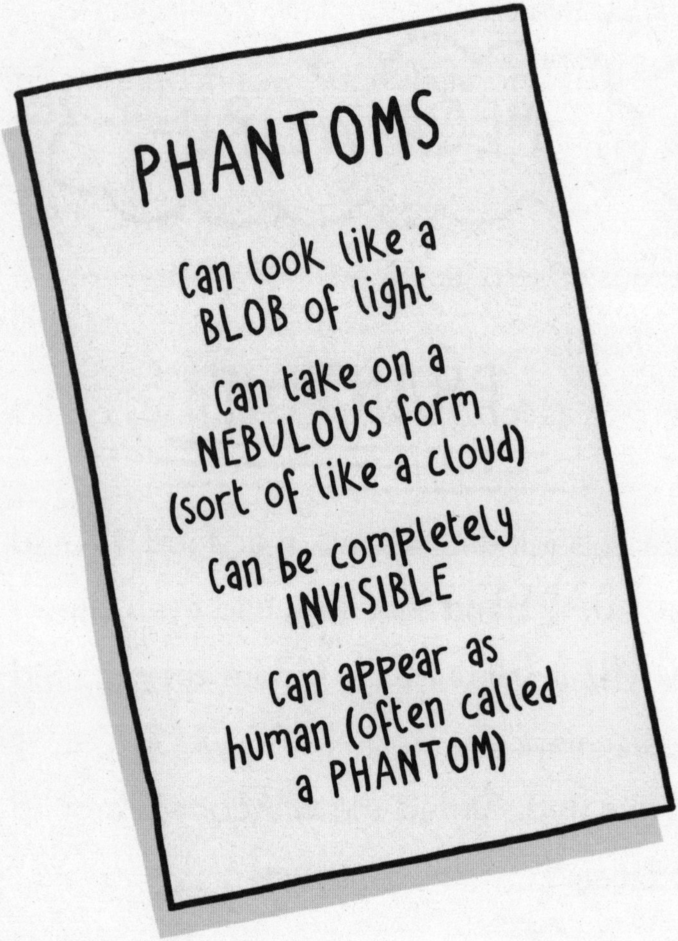

PHANTOMS

Can look like a
BLOB of light

Can take on a
NEBULOUS form
(sort of like a cloud)

Can be completely
INVISIBLE

Can appear as
human (often called
a PHANTOM)

Then Jodi said that they'd planned a MISSION and also that it was happening in one minute.

Maisie wasn't scared AT ALL when we arrived at the janitor's office.

In fact, as soon as we got there she knocked on the door really loudly.

We all knew that the LOLLIPOP man kept his LOLLIPOP stick in the janitor's office when he wasn't using it. And one time Gary Petrie even ran in and waved it about a bit and then ran out again.

But no one answered the door and that

was probably because the janitor had his little TV on REALLY loud and it was SO loud that I could actually tell that he was watching that programme where people give up their houses and jobs and coats and go live somewhere that's sunny, like Africa or Benidorm.

So Jodi knocked EVEN HARDER and the TV went silent and the door opened.

The janitor looked at us and sighed and rubbed his forehead.

And then he said, "Wait here. I'll get my plunger."

So we explained that we weren't there

about a blocked toilet and that we were here to see the LOLLIPOP man. That's when the janitor pointed outside and that's when we saw the NEW LOLLIPOP lady with her LOLLIPOP stick.

So Maisie said, "No, not that one. The other one."

And the janitor said, "Mabel there's the only one we've got now." And then he shut the door and turned the volume back up on his little TV before Maisie could say anything else.

Even though I was TERRIFIED, I said, "Maybe you should take us to where you saw him, Maisie. In case he's still there."

So Maisie grabbed my hand and we ran along the corridor, out the Big Doors and into the playground. As soon as we got outside the bell rang and everyone started making their way back into school.

But Jodi said that we should just IGNORE the bell because this was an

IMPORTANT MISSION.

Then Maisie said, "He was over there." And she pointed to the old BIKE SHED that no one uses any more since we got the new bike shed that doesn't leak or have mice.

Zach gave me a bit of a look and I knew that it was because the old bike shed is definitely the CREEPIEST place in our playground.

I had been hoping that Maisie had spotted the LOLLIPOP man next to the football pitch or the vegetable garden or somewhere nice and not creepy like that.

Maisie ran over to the old bike shed so we followed her.

Then Maisie said, "He was standing RIGHT where I'm standing now. And then he disappeared."

We all looked around for any

PHANTOM EVIDENCE.

And Jodi even got down on the ground to see if she could find a strand of grey hair or big footprints or something. But we couldn't find anything.

But then Miss Jones blew her whistle and waved at us and we saw that everyone else was already inside the school so we had to leave the

PHANTOM SITE

and go back to class.

But when we were walking back into the school I had a

WEIRD FEELING

so I turned around and looked back at the bike shed. And that's when I saw it.

A NEBULOUS CLOUD THING.

So I ran.

Unfinished Business

That night we had a meeting at Zach's house

to talk about the

NEBULOUS CLOUD.

And Zach said that we could also interview

his mum because she

 LOVED ghosts

and she knew loads about them and that her favourite film was even called GHOST.

As soon as Zach put up the

SECRET
MEETING
STAY OUT

sign on his bedroom door Jodi made me tell everyone again about what I had seen.

Jodi looked

MEGA EXCITED

and then she asked me if I was sure and I said that I **WAS** because I hadn't bumped my head like Maisie had so I knew I hadn't been

HALLUCINATING.

Zach rubbed his face for ages (which is what he does sometimes when he can't believe all the stuff we have to deal with and he's starting to get a bit STRESSED OUT).

Then Jodi said, "Izzy. This is

STRONG EVIDENCE."

And I nodded because it WAS.

Then Zach's mum knocked on the door and said that we could do the INTERVIEW now because she had finished her YOGA that she does every night after her programmes.

I felt a bit bad because we had to LIE to Zach's mum and say we were doing a GROUP TALK on GHOSTS at school because Zach said that if his mum found out there was a PHANTOM at our school then she would TOTALLY TAKE OVER THE INVESTIGATION and follow us to school every day and try to sit at our table in class and come to dinners with us and everything, because that's how much she loves phantom stuff.

But when we went into the living room to do the interview we all got a bit of a

because it looked
COMPLETELY
DIFFERENT from
how it had when
we were eating our
pasta earlier!

There were loads of
CANDLES and WEIRD
MUSIC and Zach's mum
had even changed out of her
yoga clothes into this weird,
floaty outfit and she was
dancing and waving her
arms around a bit.

So Jodi did that thing where you make a noise with your throat to let someone know that you're there and Zach's mum stopped dancing and looked a bit embarrassed (and so did Zach).

As **SOON** as the interview started, Zach's mum got **REALLY** excited and wouldn't stop talking about how **LOVELY** she thinks phantoms are and how if she ever got to meet one it would be a

DREAM COME TRUE.

And that's when Jodi asked her if she could

just stick to answering the question we were actually asking her please and she said OK.

And this is what we found out:

PHANTOMS

1. Only some people can see them (usually young children)
2. Phantoms sometimes come back to help people who have problems (they are very kind)
3. Some phantoms linger around because they have UNFINISHED BUSINESS
4. A phantom with UNFINISHED BUSINESS can't pass over into the Ghost World until they do their BUSINESS

After the interview we thanked Zach's mum and shook her hand and asked if we could have some biscuits because taking all the notes had been HARD WORK because she had talked quite a lot.

Once we got back to Zach's room, Zach said that now we knew why Maisie had seen the phantom LOLLIPOP man the most and that it was because she was the YOUNGEST.

But then Maisie said that she WASN'T the youngest, actually, and that Jodi was the youngest by ten days and Jodi nodded that she was. Maisie said that it was only because she was so SMALL that everyone always thought she was the youngest.

That's when Zach said that maybe the phantom LOLLIPOP man just THOUGHT Maisie was the youngest because she's so small and that's why he let her see him and we all agreed because even though Maisie is in Year 4 she is actually smaller than most of the Year 1s, so what Zach said made sense.

Maisie said that she STILL wasn't a hundred per cent sure that the LOLLIPOP man WAS a phantom. But then she said that IF HE WAS then maybe he'd come back to our school because he was trying help someone with their PROBLEMS, just like

Zach's mum had said. And that maybe one of the teachers had a big problem that they needed help with, like Mr Killington's broken bike or Miss Riley's weird hair.

But everyone else thought that the phantom LOLLIPOP man had some sort of

UNFINISHED BUSINESS

because he wasn't really very friendly OR helpful and he didn't really seem to like most people.

So that's when Jodi said that the INVESTIGATION was ON and that we had

TWO MAIN OBJECTIVES

(which meant we had two things we were supposed to be doing). And they were:

(1) Get PHOTOGRAPHIC EVIDENCE that the LOLLIPOP man is a PHANTOM so we can send it to the police and prove to the world that phantoms are REAL.

(2) HELP the LOLLIPOP man by finding out what his UNFINISHED BUSINESS is ASAP so he can stop haunting our school and PASS OVER to the GHOST WORLD!

Toast.
Not Ghost.

Then next day in class, me, Jodi, Maisie and Zach were trying to have a PRIVATE MEETING about the LOLLIPOP man and how we were going to COMMUNICATE with him about his UNFINISHED BUSINESS when all of a sudden a voice from behind us said, "I know someone who can help you."

We all gasped and spun around because our secret meeting had been COMPROMISED which meant that we hadn't been whispering quietly enough and that someone had OVERHEARD US talking about secret stuff!

But when we saw it was Gary Petrie we all knew that we actually **HAD** been whispering quietly enough and that Gary Petrie had just been **SPYING** on us (because that's what he's like).

So that's when Jodi started telling Gary Petrie our **COVER STORY** because Jodi always makes us come up with a cover story ever since Gary Petrie heard us talking about

WEREWOLVES

when we went camping. So me and Maisie and Zach all did the **VERY CONVINCING**

NODDING AND FACES that Jodi made us practise at her house in case our meetings were ever COMPROMISED again while she explained to Gary Petrie that we had been talking about TOAST, not ghosts.

But Gary Petrie didn't look very convinced about the TOAST. He was SMIRKING and he kept saying, "REEEEEEEALLY??" in

an annoying voice over and over again while Jodi explained she had brought toast to school for her lunch and that we were just discussing what she should spread on it.

It was OBVIOUS Gary Petrie didn't believe us so eventually Jodi just said, "FINE. What do you know?!"

Gary Petrie smiled and pulled his chair over to our table (even though we are not allowed to do that) and said, "I know someone. But it's going to cost you."

That's when Jodi pointed her ruler RIGHT at Gary Petrie's face and said that he wasn't getting a PENNY out of us!

But Gary said that he didn't WANT a penny.

Or even a POUND.

He wanted IN.

But Jodi said, "NO WAY!"

So Gary started to move his chair away REALLY slowly and said, "Oh, well. I

suppose you'll never find out about your phantom's unfinished business then."

And Maisie started tugging on Jodi's arm so Jodi sighed and said, "Gary. Wait."Jodi told Gary that he could be a SOURCE that we sometimes used to help us but that he couldn't be part of the

OFFICIAL MISSION

because the four of us were all SPECIALLY TRAINED and had LOADS of experience and that he didn't.

And Gary smiled and said, "Deal."

That's when Gary told us that he knew someone we could talk to and that she'd had

GHOST EXPERIENCES

and that some of them had even happened at THIS SCHOOL and Maisie gripped my hand under the table.

But then Gary said, "The only thing is, it might be a bit DANGEROUS."

And Jodi said, "Take us to her."

The Eagle has Landed

As **SOON** as the bell went for afternoon break, Gary Petrie walked past us and said, "THE EAGLE HAS LANDED."

We all **STARED** at Gary because we had no idea what he was talking about and also because he'd tied his tie around his head and was wearing his coat like a cape.

Then all of a sudden he ran out of the classroom. So we grabbed our coats and ran after him.

Gary led us all the way to the end of the corridor, up one flight of stairs to where the Year 5 and 6 classrooms are, along the corridor, down another set of stairs and then back along the same corridor we'd started in.

We were getting MEGA ANNOYED because Gary was OBVIOUSLY taking us NOWHERE. And I thought Jodi was going to

with anger when Gary actually STOPPED

and got in the queue for the tuck shop!

We were JUST about to turn around and go to The Den when Zach said, "Wait. Is Gary speaking to one of the Year 6s??"

And he WAS (even though the Year 6s

talk to the Year 4s, unless they're pretending to help us with our maths so they can get a certificate or something).

The Year 6 girl looked over at us, looked back at Gary, and then nodded once.

And then Gary signalled to us that we were

to follow them. So we did.

The Year 6 girl led us to the backstage bit of the assembly hall that you have to walk through a big, heavy curtain to get to.

Zach gulped and said, "This is the DANGEROUS bit, isn't it?" And I nodded because we all knew that we'd be in DEEP TROUBLE if any of the teachers found us here because it was strictly OUT OF BOUNDS.

And we'd all heard a rumour that it was also SERIOUSLY DANGEROUS and that there were at least fifty TRAP DOORS and that only the teachers knew where they were.

Maisie REFUSED to come inside because of the TRAP DOORS so we said that she could stay on the outside and be the LOOKOUT.

It was really dark backstage and I REALLY don't like it there because it's where they keep all the costumes and wigs and props

for the school plays. And it smells OLD and DUSTY and a bit HAUNTED. And even if you paid me ONE THOUSAND POUNDS I wouldn't go back there on my own.

Jodi made us all keep our backs against the wall and slide along REALLY SLOWLY to avoid TRAP DOORS.

But the Year 6 girl just walked RIGHT through the middle bit and sat down on the floor.

Then she said, "I'm Karly with a K, by the way. Just so you get it right in your article for the school newspaper. And I wouldn't mind if you wanted to record me on your phones or anything. I'm probably going to be on TV about it all soon anyway."

We looked at Gary and he winked at us and that's when we realised that Gary had LIED to Karly and told her that we were JOURNALISTS.

But we didn't say anything because we

really wanted Karly-with-a-K to tell us about her

— GHOST EXPERIENCES. —

So Zach took his phone out and pressed record.

And this is a TRANSCRIPT of our interview (which means Jodi took Zach's phone home for the night and wrote the whole interview out, word for word, for EVIDENCE):

JODI: Interview with Karly-with-a-K. Backstage assembly hall completely out-of-bounds area.

JODI: Have you ever seen a ghost, spectre, spook or phantom?

KARLY: Yes.

JODI: Are you OK? (Note: Karly has taken a tissue out of her pocket and is dabbing her eyes even though it doesn't look like there are any tears.)

KARLY: Sorry about that. I just get a bit emotional when I have to re-live my traumatic ghost experiences. My gift can feel like a curse sometimes. It's hard being as special as I am.

JODI: What do you mean, your "gift"?

KARLY: I have second sight!

JODI: What?

KARLY: I can see ghosts. (DRAMATIC PAUSE) I'm actually one of the only people in the world who can, you know. That's why they'll probably make a programme about me soon.

JODI: What did the phantoms you've seen look like?

KARLY: You don't actually see phantoms. You feel them. You just know.

JODI: So you've never actually seen a phantom?

KARLY: Yes I have!!

JODI: But you just said—

KARLY: I meant that I've seen them and I feel them!

(Note: witness is becoming aggressive.)

JODI: Have you ever seen a phantom in this school?

KARLY: Oh, yes. Lots of times.

JODI: Where?

KARLY: Um . . . well . . . I saw one a while ago in the PE changing rooms. And I've seen one in the girls' toilets before. And in the art cupboard. And the library.

JODI: What about the playground?

KARLY: No. Phantoms are always inside.

JODI: Well, one of my sources says they

saw one in the playground yesterday.

KARLY: Who??! I'm the only one at this school who has the gift!!

JODI: I can't reveal my sources. They wish to remain anonymous.

KARLY: Wait. Yes. Actually I think I might have seen a phantom in the playground yesterday. I just forgot about it until now. Where did your source say they saw it?

JODI: In the grassy bit.

KARLY: Yes!! I remember now. Yes. I saw a phantom in the grassy bit yesterday.

JODI: Actually my source saw the suspected phantom standing in front of the old bike shed.

KARLY: Then why did you say the grassy bit? Are you trying to trick me?!

JODI: You didn't see a phantom in the playground yesterday, did you?

KARLY: Yes I did! It must have moved. That's all. They can move, you know!! They float around all over the place, actually.

JODI: What did it look like?

KARLY: Um, it sort of looked liked a see-through, floating rainbow. It made me really happy.

JODI: So it didn't look like a person then?

KARLY: Wait. Yes, you're right. It did. Now

that I think about it properly it looked a bit like a young, beautiful lady ghost wearing a long colourful dress with a ribbon in her hair and…

JODI: Please let the record show that this interview was terminated at fourteen hundred hours due to the unreliability of the witness.

As soon as Jodi TERMINATED the interview, Karly got up and stormed out.

Zach said, "She was making it all up, wasn't she?"

And we all agreed that she was and that she

DEFINITELY hadn't seen the LOLLIPOP man in the playground yesterday like Maisie had.

Jodi said that when it comes to PHANTOMS, there are a lot of FAKERS out there who just PRETEND they've seen one so they can get famous and go on programmes like "MY GHOST BEST FRIEND". And that that was why we should DEFINITELY try to take a photo of the phantom to prove that WE weren't fakers.

So we all slid carefully back along the wall and out through the Big Curtain.

And now I know where the expression

"You look like you've seen a ghost!" comes from because Maisie's face was PURE WHITE and she said,

"J-J-Jack's BACK!"

Maisie pointed out of the window to the old bike shed and even though it was quite far away we could see that the

NEBULOUS CLOUD WAS BACK!

So we RAN!

The Floating LOLLIPOP Stick!

We **BURST** through the doors and out into the playground.

Jodi was WAY in front of us because she can run MEGA FAST.

When we got there, I could see there was just a tiny bit of nebulous cloud left coming from behind the bike shed.

Jodi put her finger to her lips to tell us all to be SILENT. And then she pointed to her eyes with two fingers and then at us and then back at her eyes. And we knew that meant she wanted us to watch her CLOSELY.

Then she started pointing at Zach and putting her hands up to her face and clicking her fingers like she was taking a photograph and we realised she wanted Zach's phone

so she could try to take a photo of the
PHANTOM.

So Zach gave Jodi his phone and then he
looked at me and whispered, "Do you smell
that?" And I nodded because I did and it sort
of smelled like smoke but not smoke that
I've ever smelled before. It was weird (and a
bit disgusting).

And that's when Jodi yelled,

and leaped around the back of the bike shed

and started taking loads of pictures.

But there was no one there. The

NEBULOUS CLOUD

was GONE.

Then all of a sudden the FIRE ALARM went off and we all covered our ears and

SCREAMED

and EVERYONE ELSE in the playground started screaming too, even though that is the EXACT OPPOSITE of what we have been trained to do when the fire alarm goes off.

Maisie fainted INSTANTLY so me and Zach picked her up by an arm and leg each because that's what we always do during a FIRE DRILL even though Miss Jones tells us exactly when it is going to happen and that there's NOTHING TO WORRY ABOUT.

Once we were all lined up at the FIRE ASSEMBLY POINT and Mr Graves, the head teacher, had ticked all our names off the list to make sure no one was still inside, he told us through his MEGAPHONE that everyone was to STAY STILL and STAY IN LINE until the FIRE FIGHTERS got here because this was

NOT A DRILL.

LOADS of people were panicking and crying because they'd left stuff in the classrooms that they were scared was going to get

BURNED TO A CRISP

like their favourite pencil case or a book
they'd been reading and Gary Petrie kept
going on about his MONSTER MUNCH.

And then it started to rain and EVERYONE
began screaming again and Gary Petrie said
that he felt NAKED because he was only
wearing a shirt and not a jumper and the rain
had made his shirt a bit SEE-THROUGH.
And Mr Graves had to use his megaphone
LOADS to try to calm everyone down.

And **THAT'S** when I saw it.

I couldn't believe it!

A FLOATING
LOLLIPOP STICK!

It was floating **RIGHT ALONG THE BOTTOM CORRIDOR!**

Just then we heard **SIRENS** and the fire fighters all rushed in and did a **FULL SEARCH**. Then the main fire fighter came over and told Mr Graves that there was no one left inside the school and also that there was **NO FIRE**.

Everyone started

CHEERING

when the fire fighter said that and Gary Petrie punched the air and some of the Year 6 girls started hugging each other and crying.

But me and Jodi and Zach and Maisie just all **STARED** at each other.

Because we knew that fire alarms don't just set themselves off.

But then all of a sudden Zach gasped and said, "What if the

NEBULOUS CLOUD

went inside the school to get its LOLLIPOP STICK and set off the SMOKE ALARM?"

And we all GASPED because we knew Zach was right!

Knock Once for Yes, Twice for No

The next day, Zach told us that he'd found out **MORE** about ghosts from his mum and that she had burned his toast that morning and the smell had reminded him about the

WEIRD SMOKE SMELL

behind the old bike shed.

So Zach said that he asked his mum if phantoms have a SMELL and she said that they DID and that when phantoms let you SMELL THEM it means that they are trying to

COMMUNICATE WITH YOU.

Maisie GASPED and said, "The nebulous cloud thing smelled really weird!" and Zach nodded and said that it did and that sometimes the only way you know a ghost is around is because you smell a weird

UNEXPLAINED SMELL.

Then Zach said that the phantom was OBVIOUSLY trying to communicate with us and that he must need our help to do his UNFINISHED BUSINESS.

And THAT'S when Maisie said that we needed to find out what the SMELL meant so that we could help him. But none of us had any idea what the smell meant because we didn't know how to read smells.

And that's when Zach said, "You're not going to like this. But I think we need Karly-with-a-K's help."

Jodi was **NOT** happy when Zach asked Gary Petrie to ask Karly if she'd sit with us at lunch because Jodi was ONE HUNDRED PER CENT convinced that Karly was a PHANTOM FAKER.

But Zach said that she might **NOT** be and that she might actually know how to communicate with phantoms and DECODE SMELLS.

Just then someone cleared their throat really loudly, and we looked up and saw Karly was standing there with her tray. And so was Gary Petrie.

Karly looked at Gary and Gary said, "Karly

has agreed to have a lunch meeting with you to discuss how sorry you are." And that's when Jodi gave Zach a LOOK and Zach just sort of stared down at his chicken nuggets because he knew Jodi was

FURIOUS

that he had said she would APOLOGISE to Karly for saying she was making it all up.

Karly smirked a bit and looked RIGHT at Jodi and I thought FOR SURE that Jodi was going to say something BAD to Karly. But she didn't.

She looked right back at Karly and said, "I'm sorry I called you an unreliable witness."

And I was

SHOCKED.

Because Jodi NEVER apologises. Even when she is one hundred per cent WRONG! And I knew that she must have done it because she knew how important it was that we help the LOLLIPOP man.

Karly smiled and said, "Thank you." And

then she sat down and started eating her salad and I knew that the **WHOLE DINNER HALL** was **STARING** at us because a Year 6 was eating lunch with a bunch of Year 4s.

Then Gary Petrie sat down too (even though no one had asked him to) and I thought I was going to be **SICK** because he opened a bag of Monster Munch and starting dipping

them in his soup.

Then Karly said, "I hear you need my help to communicate with the other side?"

And we all nodded that we did.

Karly smiled and said, "I'm not surprised you asked for my help. I assume you've all heard of the Karly Method?"

But none of us had so we didn't say

anything.

Then Karly said, "I discovered it when I was just a baby and it's probably the best way of communicating with the Ghost World that you can get."

I had **NO IDEA** what the **KARLY METHOD** was but then all of a sudden Karly started **KNOCKING** on the table with her right fist. Then her left. Then her right. And then she closed her eyes and put both hands on her shoulders and said, "Is anybody there?"

I looked at Jodi and she rolled her eyes.

Karly kept her eyes shut for ages and I wasn't really sure what was supposed to be

happening but then all of a sudden there was a loud knock on the table. I looked at Karly, but she still had her hands on her shoulders.

Then Karly said, "Knock once for yes and twice for no. OK?"

And we heard one knock. Zach's eyes went WIDE and Maisie gripped my hand.

Then Karly said, "Welcome, um..." And then she opened one eye and said, "What's the name of your phantom again?"

And Zach said, "LOLLIPOP man."

And Karly said, "Yes. I can feel that."

I didn't really know what that meant but then Karly said, "Are you the phantom

LOLLIPOP man?"

And then we heard ONE KNOCK and we all knew that that meant YES.

I looked around and saw that Jodi was STARING at Karly. And so was Zach and I was starting to feel a bit faint because this was SERIOUSLY SCARY and also because Maisie was now sitting on my knee and she was pressing against my chest.

Then Karly said, "We're here to help you. Would you like us to help you?"

And we heard TWO KNOCKS, which meant NO.

That's when Karly opened her eyes and

said, "Are you sure, Mr LOLLIPOP Man?"

And the phantom LOLLIPOP man knocked TWICE which meant NO and we were all a bit confused.

Then all of a sudden Mrs Kidd, the moany dinner monitor, came over and told us to stop BANGING on the table or ELSE. And then she bent down and asked Gary Petrie what he thought he was doing under the table.

Jodi narrowed her eyes at Gary Petrie when he said he was looking for a Monster Munch that he'd dropped and I could tell she thought he'd been doing the knocking.

When Mrs Kidd had gone, Karly said, "Your

phantom obviously doesn't want your help. Some of them are just like that. You should probably just leave him alone."

That's when Maisie looked up at me and grabbed my face with both her hands. And I knew that there was **NO WAY** she was going to let us leave the phantom **LOLLIPOP** man alone!

Give Maisie
CAKE!

As soon as we finished lunch we ran to The Den.

Zach wanted to try the Karly Method again and that's when Jodi said Karly-with-a-K was definitely a fake and it had been Gary Petrie all along. And we knew she was right.

And then Jodi said that we needed a **NEW PLAN** and that the **NEW PLAN** was to interview the

WHOLE SCHOOL

so that we could find out what the phantom **LOLLIPOP** man's **UNFINISHED BUSINESS** was.

So I said that we should interview **STAFF ONLY** because the **LOLLIPOP** man never really spoke to pupils. And everyone agreed and I quickly made a list of everyone that worked in the school and put **THE OFFICE**

LADIES at the very top.

But then Jodi picked up another pen and put a line through that because we'd already spoken to them (and also because she finds it hard not to TAKE OVER when other people are doing stuff).

So I said that Jodi shouldn't have done that because we had only asked the office ladies where the LOLLIPOP man WAS and not about his UNFINISHED BUSINESS. And Jodi didn't say anything back because she knew that I was right and she was wrong.

So we went looking for Mrs McManus, the Year 6 teacher, and we found her in her room eating sweets at her desk and when we asked her if we could speak to her about the LOLLIPOP man she looked a bit

NERVOUS

but she said yes.

We asked Mrs McManus loads of questions like, "Do you know if the LOLLIPOP man was learning to play the drums?" and "Had he already booked his summer holiday?" and "Do you know if he was doing a 1000-piece jigsaw before he died??"

Because we thought that those were

the types of things the LOLLIPOP man might have started and not been able to finish and like Zach said, you'd probably be really annoyed if you'd almost finished a 1000-piece jigsaw and then you died.

But Mrs McManus didn't know the answer to ANY of the questions we asked her. And Zach said that he didn't think Mrs McManus knew ANYTHING about the LOLLIPOP man. And that's when I remembered that Miss Jones hadn't even seemed to know WHO the LOLLIPOP man WAS and we all thought it was a bit sad because he'd been at our school for YEARS.

So we knew we HAD to ask the OFFICE LADIES because they DID know the LOLLIPOP MAN and if anyone would know about his BUSINESS, it would be them.

But the office ladies were all on their way to the staff room to have their lunch and even though we said, "EXCUSE ME" really loud, four times, they just kept on walking and ignored us. But Maisie said that we COULDN'T GIVE UP and then she grabbed my hand and started running after the office ladies.

When we got to the staff room the door was closed, and even though we knocked

REALLY LOUD no one answered. And we could hear MUSIC and

coming from inside and then everyone started singing, "HAPPY BIRTHDAY TO YOOOOOU!"

We were all shocked because we didn't know that the school did birthday parties in the staff room. And WE'D definitely never been invited to one!

Then all of a sudden the door opened and Mr Killington came out and said, "OH! What are you four doing here? Is everything OK?"

And we said that it was.

But then all of a sudden Maisie

COLLAPSED!

But it wasn't like it usually is when she faints because this one was really quick and she was still COMPLETELY AWAKE and saying, "I feel weak. I feel weak, weak, WEAK."

Mr Killington told us to help him lift Maisie and take her into the staff room and lie her down on one of the couches, so we did.

Then Maisie said, "I forgot to eat breakfast. I need FOOD."

So Mr Killington rushed over to where the birthday cake was and cut Maisie a

HUGE

slice and THAT'S when Maisie looked
up and

WINKED

at us!

We all

because we knew that there was NOTHING **WRONG** with Maisie and that she was just **FAKING IT**.

I had

why Maisie had FAKE FAINTED because she'd never done that before.

Zach asked her if it was because she wanted a bit of birthday cake and I thought that that might be right because Maisie

LOVES cakes

and she's always baking with her mum.

But Maisie said that it WASN'T about the cake (even though she wouldn't stop eating it and she didn't offer anyone else a bit even though Zach was practically DROOLING). Maisie said that she did it so we could get

inside the STAFF ROOM and ask the office
ladies about the LOLLIPOP man.

Jodi smiled and said,

"Maisie Millar. You.

Are. A.

GENIUS!"

And Maisie smiled and kept on eating the
cake.

Then Mr Killington came back with juice
for Maisie, and he'd brought more cake for
us too!

And we knew that it must be HIS birthday

because he seemed to be able to make all the decisions about the cake. So we said happy birthday to him and he said thanks and told us we could stay for a bit until Maisie felt better.

Then Miss Jones and loads of the other teachers came over to see if Maisie was OK and she did a weak little nod and made her eyes look heavy and I had to cover my mouth a bit so I didn't laugh because it was really funny seeing Maisie pretend like that.

Miss Ross asked if there was anything she could do to help Maisie and Maisie said, "Yes, actually. You could help us with our poster for the LOLLIPOP man's funeral."

Miss Ross looked a bit

SHOCKED

when Maisie said that and we knew that it was because she was another person who didn't know about the LOLLIPOP man MOVING ON.

Miss Ross asked us if we were SURE the LOLLIPOP man had died and we said that we were and that the office ladies had told us.

Miss Ross and some of the other teachers asked us about our funeral poster and Maisie told them that we needed to know more about the LOLLIPOP man's life for the poster and then we asked them our questions.

But **NO ONE** was able to tell us **ANYTHING** about the **LOLLIPOP** man's life when he wasn't lollipopping! It was **WEIRD**.

So that's when Jodi whispered, "Maybe we should ask where the **LOLLIPOP** man went in the school when he wasn't lollipopping. So we can go there and try to **COMMUNICATE** with him about his unfinished business."

So I said, "Does anyone know where the **LOLLIPOP** man's favourite place in the school was?"

And all the teachers just sort of looked at each other but they didn't say anything.

Then Jodi said, "It's for a **POEM** we're

doing."

And I gave Jodi a LOOK because we hadn't said ANYTHING about a POEM and now I knew that we were going to have to do a poster AND a poem so that all the teachers wouldn't find out that we were LYING to them.

That's when Mr Killington said, "I don't actually remember seeing the LOLLIPOP man anywhere other than at the crossing outside the school."

And then the other teachers all nodded and said the same.

So that's when me and Jodi took a deep breath and went over to the office ladies

who were sitting in the NICEST bit of the staff room, next to the heater.

But they wouldn't even LISTEN to our questions about what the LOLLIPOP man got up to when he wasn't lollipopping OR where his favourite place in the school had been and they just started TUTTING and SHAKING THEIR HEADS at us and saying that it was

RIDICULOUS

that the teachers had allowed PUPILS into the staff room at break time and how the whole school was going DOWNHILL.

I got a bit annoyed with the office ladies when they said that because even though we were only doing a FAKE poster for the LOLLIPOP man's funeral, THEY didn't know that, and it wasn't very nice not to want to help someone do a FUNERAL POSTER. And before I realised what I was doing I said most of that to them OUT LOUD and when I'd finished I looked at Jodi and she looked the

MOST SHOCKED I HAVE EVER SEEN HER.

I didn't know **WHAT** was going to happen because **NO ONE** ever stands up to the office ladies when they're being mean, not even Mr Graves!

I gulped and waited for someone to tell me that I was

EXPELLED

from the school for **LIFE**. But that's not what happened.

What happened was that all the office ladies stopped drinking their tea and eating their cake and just looked down at the ground for a bit.

And then one of them said, "We're sorry. We didn't realise that you'd been allowed in here to raise money for funeral arrangements. Here you go."

And **THAT'S** when all the office ladies started to give us money and I had **NO IDEA** what to do but Jodi gave me a **LOOK** that meant "JUST SMILE AND TAKE THE MONEY SO YOU DON'T GET EXPELLED!"

So we started collecting the money and saying thank you.

And Jodi said, "Thank you for your kind donations. This will help us to buy a special PLAQUE in the LOLLIPOP man's memory. We'd like to hang the plaque in the LOLLIPOP man's favourite place in the school. Do any of you know where he liked to go when he wasn't lollipopping?"

I couldn't BELIEVE Jodi was asking them more questions when I'd almost just been EXPELLED! And I ALSO couldn't believe that she kept on ADDING to the list of all the stuff we had to make!

The office ladies all looked at each other and then the main one said, "Um … we're not sure. Maybe you could just put it up outside the school, next to the front entrance?"

Jodi said that that was a

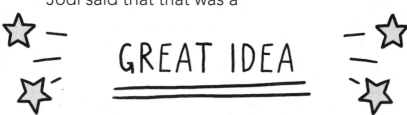

GREAT IDEA

and then she shook everyone's hand and made me do the same.

And when we were walking away Jodi whispered, "This is going to be more difficult than we thought. Even the OFFICE LADIES don't know where the LOLLIPOP man used to go when he wasn't out on the road!"

So we went back over to where Maisie and Zach were and someone had given them MORE birthday cake.

And THAT'S when I noticed that not EVERYONE who worked at our school was at the Staff Room Birthday Party. So I said, "Stop eating the cake!!"

Because I knew that we were all going to have to have COMPLETELY EMPTY STOMACHS for the next part of the

PHANTOM MISSION.

NEVER
Anger a
Dinner Lady!

Lunch was almost over by the time we got back to the dining hall.

But we rushed up to the counter anyway and asked for SECONDS and we made sure we were REALLY NICE to all the dinner ladies (even the mean one) and we kept saying

stuff like, "Everything smells DELICIOUS!"
and "Yes, PLEASE!" and "BRAVO!" We all
made sure that we ate

EVERY SINGLE SCRAP

of food on our plates and said,
"MMMMMMMMMHHH!" really loud and rubbed
our stomachs until the dinner
ladies looked over at us.

Then Zach picked
up his plate and
started licking it, just
like we'd planned.

We waited until all the other pupils left and then we went up to the serving bit and asked if we could interview one of the dinner ladies for a school project (because we knew the dinner ladies would tell us they were busy and to go away if we just started asking them about the LOLLIPOP man so we had to be SNEAKY).

But then the MEANEST DINNER LADY came over and said, "What project?!" and I started panicking a bit.

So that's when Maisie said, "It's about the history of our school. We want to know more about the history of school dinners."

I looked at Jodi and she raised her eyebrows because sometimes Maisie

COMPLETELY SURPRISES

us and comes up with a really good COVER STORY out of NOWHERE.

So I said, "Um, yes. Because if we didn't have food then we wouldn't be able to LEARN so school dinners is probably the most important part of the WHOLE SCHOOL."

The mean dinner lady stared at us for a minute. And then all of a sudden she actually SMILED A BIT and said, "Well. I can't argue with THAT. Back you come."

The dinner lady disappeared into the kitchen and we sort of stood there SHOCKED until Zach eventually said, "Did that just happen?! Did she just say we could go into the kitchen?!" And I nodded and Zach said,

And he was RIGHT to say WOW because pupils are NEVER allowed to go into the kitchen EVER!

So we pushed the kitchen doors open and walked in and it was SO WEIRD to be in a bit of the school that we had never been in before and we couldn't stop looking at EVERYTHING like the HUGE FREEZER and the MASSIVE SPOONS and the dinner ladies were all working so hard and fast at doing the washing up that they looked a bit like ROBOTS!

The dinner lady told us to follow her into the back, so we did. And then she pointed to some upturned buckets and told us to sit down. That's when Jodi nudged me and I realised that the interview had started and that it was UP TO ME to do this interview PROFESSIONALLY and make sure we got the information we needed.

Jodi passed me the pad and pen, and she squeezed my hand a bit when she did it and I knew it meant GOOD LUCK.

So I looked at the notepad and PRETENDED that there were questions about

THE
HISTORY
OF THE
SCHOOL

on there, even though there weren't any.

So I asked the dinner lady how long she had been a dinner lady and she told us that she had worked at the school for over

TWENTY-FIVE YEARS

and I was a bit surprised because that's AGES to work in just one place and I had NO IDEA she loved being a dinner lady so much because she always looks

REALLY GRUMPY.

Then the dinner lady started saying loads of stuff about things being better in the OLD DAYS and that now you weren't even allowed to butter a slice of TOAST without asking someone's permission or filling in a FORM.

So I nodded loads and pretended to be writing everything down, but I didn't write anything. But then the dinner lady wouldn't stop talking about PAPER TOWELS and I wasn't sure what to say to make her stop until I got a

BRILLIANT IDEA.

So I said, "Everyone else we've spoken to said that they think being a LOLLIPOP man is the MOST IMPORTANT job in the school. What do you think?"

And THAT'S when the dinner lady's face went BRIGHT RED. And she shouted, "WHAT?!"

Zach gulped and moved his bucket back a bit and I wiped my face because the dinner lady had actually SPAT on it a bit.

The dinner lady got up off her bucket and started waving her arms around and shouting, "All that man does is STAND STILL!! He should try coming back HERE

for EIGHT HOURS A DAY!!" We all watched as the dinner lady kept on shouting. And then some of the OTHER dinner ladies came over and she told them what I'd said and THEY all started shouting about the LOLLIPOP man and about how all he does is "OCCASIONALLY WALK ACROSS THE ROAD" and that most of the time he's "NOWHERE TO BE SEEN!"

Then Jodi said, "Um. Time to go, Izzy!" but I didn't move because even though the dinner ladies were TOTALLY FREAKING OUT, we were in the middle of a VITAL INTERVIEW.

But then I noticed that the only reason Maisie was still sitting on her bucket was because Jodi was holding her up. And also that Maisie was starting to SLIP.

But I just KNEW that I could squeeze in a REAL question before Maisie slid off her bucket completely.

So I said, "Where does the LOLLIPOP man go when he's nowhere to be seen?"

And one of the dinner ladies looked RIGHT AT ME and said, "He sneaks off to the LIBRARY for a NAP, of course!"

And I looked at Zach and he smiled because we'd just found out where the phantom LOLLIPOP man LURKED!

But then Jodi said, "Izzy! We REEEEALLY need to go!!!"

So we all said thank you to the dinner lady and dragged Maisie into the playground for some fresh air.

And that's when Jodi said that Maisie

didn't faint because of all the

DINNER LADY SHOUTING.

She said that Maisie had fainted because she had seen the phantom LOLLIPOP man again!

And THAT'S when I noticed that Jodi's face had gone COMPLETELY WHITE.

And she said, "I think I saw him TOO!"

Strange Unexplained Smells

Before I had a chance to say ANYTHING, Jodi grabbed Zach's phone and RAN.

I looked at Zach and he looked at me and said, "GO! I'll stay with Maisie."

So I ran after Jodi, all the way along the bottom corridor, past the head teacher's office and out into the school car park.

But the phantom LOLLIPOP man was gone.

Jodi pointed across the car park towards the road and said, "He was right there. I saw him through the kitchen window."

So that's when I shouted, "LIBRARY! NOW!" and turned and ran back in to the school.

But the library was LOCKED and we knew that probably meant that Mrs Bottery, the librarian, had gone to buy more Charity Chocolate from the Year 6s because Zach says that she is OBSESSED with it.

I was just about to say we should go and get Zach and Maisie and come back in ten minutes when Jodi completely FLOPPED on to the ground.

At first I thought she'd FAINTED because of the way she fell, but then I saw that her eyes were WIDE OPEN and I remembered that this was one of Jodi's MOVES for when you need to duck down quickly so no one sees you.

And that's when I realised that there must be someone or SOMETHING inside the library!

So I FLOPPED on to the ground too and waited for Jodi to say what to do next.

But then we heard a voice say, "What are you DOING?"And we looked up and saw it was the librarian. And she was eating a bar of chocolate which meant that Zach was right about her being OBSESSED because she obviously couldn't even wait until she got back to her desk to eat it.

So I just said that we had been lying down

waiting for her to come back because we were feeling tired after our lunch and the librarian just sort of shook her head at us and told us to go inside. I was

because as much as I like the library, it's a bit **SPOOKY** in there because it's in the **VERY OLDEST** part of the school.

Jodi waited until the librarian went behind her desk and then she whispered, "I think I saw someone standing behind that bookcase over there. Follow me."

So I took a DEEP BREATH and followed Jodi as she snuck through the bookcases to the other side of the library.

But there was no one behind the bookcase and we couldn't see any nebulous clouds or anything like that so Jodi said that the phantom LOLLIPOP man must have gone into

FULL INVISIBLE FORM.

Then all of a sudden, Jodi FROZE and said, "Can you smell that?" And that's when I smelled a weird smell that was sort of like oranges and perfume.

We both walked around, sniffing the air, trying to figure out what the smell was and that's when Jodi said that the smell was getting STRONGER.

Then all of a sudden Jodi said, "I think it's coming from that chair!"

Jodi got a

REALLY WEIRD

look on her face but I wasn't sure why. So I walked over and sat down on the chair and sniffed the armrest and the smell was

REALLY STRONG there so I said, "You're right. It's the chair. It sort of smells a bit like Christmas. It's weird."

But when I looked back up at Jodi she had Zach's phone in her hand and she was pointing it RIGHT AT ME.

So I said, "What are you doing?"

And Jodi said, "Stay **PERFECTLY STILL**."

And that's when I remembered about the **STRANGE UNEXPLAINED SMELLS**.

And I realised what was going on. Jodi was trying to get

PHOTOGRAPHIC EVIDENCE.

I was sitting on top of a **PHANTOM!**

Ghost Burns & Holey Tights

Before I knew what was happening I was in The Den.

Zach and Maisie were there too and they were saying something to me but I couldn't really hear what they were saying because my head was SPINNING and I had NO

IDEA how I even got there! Then all of a sudden, Jodi

into The Den and she looked PURE WHITE. And THAT'S when I remembered what had happened in the library and how I had SAT ON A PHANTOM!!

Jodi STARED into my eyes and asked if I was OK and if my bottom or legs or anything felt weird because of sitting on top of a ghost.

And Zach said, "What HAPPENED?!"

So Jodi explained about the STRANGE UNEXPLAINED SMELL and the old library chair in the far corner of the library and how I had accidentally sat right on top of the PHANTOM LOLLIPOP MAN.

Jodi said that I had looked a bit like I'd fainted but that I'd still managed to get up and run all the way to The Den before we had a chance to try to communicate with him.

I told Jodi that I didn't remember doing **ANY** of that and Jodi nodded and held my hand and said that I was in

and the body can do STRANGE THINGS

when it's in SHOCK.

Then Zach asked me if I had been BURNED by the ghost and I said, "WHAT?!" Because we had

NO IDEA

that you could get a GHOST BURN!!

And that's when Maisie said, "We found out something."

And then she asked to see my legs so I showed her. But Maisie said that she was going to have to CUT A HOLE IN MY TIGHTS to be sure. So I just sort of nodded and Maisie took her pencil case out of her bag and started cutting LOADS of holes in my tights so she could see my legs and Jodi held my hand while she did it because she knew I was scared about the whole GHOST BURN THING.

But Maisie said that my legs looked

COMPLETELY NORMAL

except for the fact that I now had loads of holes in my tights.

And that's when Zach told us that he and Maisie had bumped into Karly-with-a-K on the way to The Den and that she had been CRYING because she'd just seen a PHANTOM run through the playground and that it bumped into her a bit and made her arm go ICE COLD.

Jodi rolled her eyes and said that Karly was

obviously just making it up.

But then Maisie said, "She had evidence."

That's when Maisie told us that Karly had made both Maisie and Zach touch her arm and that it HAD been cold. In fact, it had been ICE COLD. And that Karly had said that it hurt to be touched and that she thought it was an ICE BURN.

And I know all about ice burns, because one time I found an ice lolly at the very back of our freezer, and it had been there for so long that its wrapper had fallen off or disintegrated or something, and it was SO COLD that the minute I put it in my mouth it STUCK right to my tongue and I started screaming because I couldn't get it off and it was REALLY PAINFUL. And when my dad eventually managed to get it off he said that I had an ICE BURN on my tongue! And I didn't even know that you could get an ice burn until that happened.

So anyway, I didn't have any burns on my legs and Jodi said that I should go to the toilet and check that I didn't have any on my bottom. But I said that I wasn't doing that and that my bottom felt fine and that I didn't feel cold or burned at ALL.

Maisie said that it was probably because

I was wearing thick tights and a skirt that I'd managed to avoid a GHOST BURN and that Karly had only been wearing a short-sleeved shirt when the phantom LOLLIPOP man had bumped into her. That's when Zach said that we all had to come to school wearing

GHOST PROTECTION SUITS

from now on and Maisie nodded LOADS.

Then Jodi said, "Um. I think there's

something wrong with your phone, Zach. It's DOING SOMETHING!"

And we all turned and looked at Jodi and she was holding out Zach's phone and it was making a weird SCREECHY sound.

Zach said, "Why is it doing that? What did you do to it?!"

But Jodi said that she didn't do **ANYTHING** and that she'd only tried to take a photo of me sitting on top of the phantom **LOLLIPOP** man in the library.

That's when Zach gasped and put his hand on his head and said, "**OH NO!** Maybe that's why people **FAKE** ghost photos all the time. Maybe something goes

if you ever catch a **REAL** ghost on camera.

Maybe the camera can't handle all the PHANTOM ENERGY or something and it explodes. DON'T MOVE!"

So Jodi FROZE.

Zach said that we needed to stay PERFECTLY STILL and that meant Maisie couldn't faint.

So I told Maisie to think about all the stuff that DIDN'T make her want to faint and Maisie nodded and said that she would think of MARSHMALLOWS and CAKES and HUMPBACK WHALES because she likes all those things.

Then Zach started walking towards Jodi

reeeeeeeeeeally slooooooooowly because he said that he needed to try to STOP the phone from exploding. And then he said that he might be able to stop the whole thing by pressing the OFF BUTTON.

Maisie shut her eyes tight and began chewing on nothing with her mouth wide open and I knew that she had gone to her HAPPY PLACE in her head and that she was probably pretending that she was at home in her kitchen with her mum eating loads of cakes.

I held my breath as Zach got closer and closer to the phone and I could see that Jodi was actually SWEATING.

Then when Zach was almost there he reached out his shaky finger and pressed the OFF button.

And that's when The Den went completely BLACK.

Blackout!

At first there was just silence.

Then I heard something and I realised that it was Maisie and that she was still doing the chewing thing and that she must not have even REALISED that it had gone PITCH BLACK in The Den.

And Jodi said, "Izzy?"

And Zach said, "Is everyone OK? Why isn't Maisie screaming?"

And Jodi said, "BAD mistake, Zach."

And that's when Maisie must have opened her eyes because she started screaming, "I can't open my eyes... I CAN'T OPEN MY EYES!!!"

So I used my most SOOTHING VOICE to tell Maisie that she COULD open her eyes and the reason she couldn't see was because the lights had gone out in The Den.

Then all of a sudden the lights came back on and Zach started yelling, "I DID IT! LOOK! I DID IT!"

And we saw that Zach's phone was still there and that it hadn't exploded.

Zach said that taking a picture of a REAL ghost must have caused the phone to FREAK OUT and caused a BLACK OUT and that it had probably affected the WHOLE SCHOOL and maybe even the whole country!

Maisie said that we should never EVER turn the phone on EVER again because she was TERRIFIED of the dark.

But Jodi said that we needed to find a way to get the phone working without exploding so she could print the PHANTOM PHOTO at home and give it to the police because it was

REAL
PHANTOM
EVIDENCE.

And that's when Maisie said, "FORGET about the picture. We've got more important things to focus on. We need to go back to the library and find out what the phantom LOLLIPOP man's unfinished business is

NOW before he floats away!"

So we ran.

On the Run!

On the way to the library we heard someone shout, "STOP RUNNING THIS INSTANT!" And we all stopped and turned around and saw that it was Mrs Seith the scary deputy head.

Jodi whispered that we should all just keep

running. But none of us did. Not even Jodi because Mrs Seith is **SERIOUSLY SCARY**. And we heard that one time she made every single parent cry at Parents' Evening. That's how scary she is.

So we all just started walking towards the library really slowly so that Mrs Seith would go away. But then we heard her

GASP

and I thought that maybe she'd just seen the PHANTOM. But then she said, "ISABELLA! What ON EARTH have you done to your TIGHTS!"

And that's when I remembered about all the holes that Maisie had cut in my tights and also that pupils are NOT ALLOWED to cut holes in their tights OR draw on their legs after all the Year 6s did it last year and there was an assembly about it. Then the bell went and Mrs Seith told the others to go to class and that I was to STAY EXACTLY WHERE I WAS.

I had to wait there for AGES while Mrs

Seith went outside to shout at everyone for not standing in line properly. And then when she came back into the school she went into one of the classrooms for ages and my legs were starting to get sore from standing in the same place for so long so I was just about to sit down when I noticed **HOW COLD** my legs were. I touched them with my hand to make sure and they were

FREEZING.

But there weren't any ghost burns. And that's when I noticed that I could feel a

BREEZE and I gasped because

I just **KNEW**

that the phantom LOLLIPOP man was NEAR.

And that's when I turned around and saw it, leaning against the wall.

The phantom LOLLIPOP man's LOLLIPOP STICK!

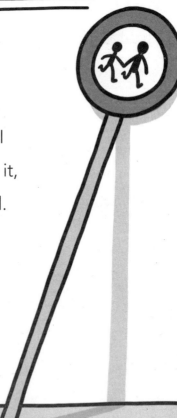

I ran all the way to class. I didn't even CARE
that Mrs Seith would be after me. There was
NO WAY I was going to stand, alone, in
that corridor with a PHANTOM and try to
communicate with it about its

UNFINISHED BUSINESS.

But when I walked into the classroom, Miss
Jones took one look at my tights and told
me to stand outside in the corridor and that
she'd be out to speak to me in a minute.

I looked through the glass bit of the door

and started waving my hands ALL OVER
the place to get Zach's attention. And when
he looked I breathed on the glass and drew
a LOLLIPOP STICK and an ARROW
pointing down the corridor and Zach's eyes
went WIDE and he nudged Jodi and she
looked at me and gave me a SALUTE and

I knew that meant that she was about to do something

VERY RISKY.

Jodi whispered something to Zach and Maisie and then put up her hand and said something to Miss Jones. And then Miss Jones nodded and handed Jodi the TOILET PASS.

Then Jodi came out into the corridor and said, "Let's go!"

But I said that if Miss Jones came out to speak to me and I wasn't here then I would be in DEEP trouble because I was already ON THE RUN from the scary deputy head!

But Jodi just smiled and said, "Don't worry. Miss Jones won't get a chance to come out and speak to you for at LEAST ten minutes."

And then Jodi pointed into the classroom and Maisie gave me a THUMBS-UP and I knew that she was about to cause a

MAJOR DISTRACTION

like she had done in the staff room.

Then Jodi said, "Where's the LOLLIPOP stick?"

So I grabbed her arm and took her back down the bottom corridor.

It was GONE. But thanks to the dinner ladies, we knew EXACTLY where the LOLLIPOP man would be heading. The LIBRARY!

Jodi said that if we got there quick we could HIDE and wait until we smelled the

WEIRD SMELL

and saw the chair cushion moving a bit and that then she would do the KARLY METHOD to COMMUNICATE with him.

So we RAN down the corridor as FAST as we could and when we got there Jodi made us get down on the ground and crawl so that Mrs Bottery the librarian didn't notice us because we didn't have a LIBRARY PASS

That's when Mrs Bottery's phone rang and Jodi whispered, "This is our chance."

And then she did a DROP AND ROLL under one of the bookshelves and I did the same. And even though it had been AGES since we did our DROP AND ROLL TRAINING at Jodi's house my body just

seemed to know exactly what to do without me even thinking about it. And Jodi says that that's called MUSCLE MEMORY and it means that your actual muscles remember how to do something even when your brain forgets and that's why Jodi makes us practise all her moves FIFTY TIMES IN A ROW.

So then we COMMANDO-CRAWLED all the way to the back corner of the library and hid behind one of the bookcases and waited for the phantom LOLLIPOP man to arrive and sit in his chair.

But then Mrs Bottery said, "HELLO?? Is there someone there??" I looked at Jodi and she put a finger to her lips.

But then Mrs Bottery said, "If there's someone here you'd better say now. I'm about to lock up for the day!"

And I looked at Jodi with my WIDE EYES

because I did **NOT** want to get locked in the library **AGAIN** like the time with the **DEMON DINNER LADIES.**

I was just about to tell Jodi we needed to **ABORT THE MISSION** when I heard a

And Jodi whispered, "That's a ghost sound!!"

And then I smelled the **WEIRD SMELL!!**

And Jodi must have smelled it too because her eyes went **WIDE.**

Jodi looked at me and I looked at Jodi and

I knew that she was trying to decide whether we should run so we didn't get locked in the library overnight or whether we should stay and try to communicate with the phantom.

Then I heard Mrs Bottery put the key in the lock and I almost

FAINTED WITH RELIEF

when Jodi said, "Run!"

We RAN through the library shouting, "DON'T LOCK US IN!"

Mrs Bottery looked a bit shocked when she saw us. And then she said, "Oh, thank

GOODNESS it's just you two. I SWEAR I've been hearing strange noises in here for WEEKS."

We tried to leave but that's when Mrs Bottery said, "Wait. What are you two doing in here anyway? I didn't see you come in. Do you have a library pass to be out of class?"

So Jodi took the TOILET PASS out of her pocket and flashed it really quickly. And even though a toilet pass is not a library pass, it's the same COLOUR as a library pass, so Jodi just took a chance.

And it WORKED!

But then Mrs Bottery asked us loads of questions about what books we had been looking at and if she could help us quickly before she locked up.

So Jodi said that we'd been looking for a POEM to read at the LOLLIPOP man's funeral.

And that's when the librarian got a bit upset because she said that she hadn't known that Jack had passed away. And I noticed that she was the only one (except for Maisie) who seemed to know the LOLLIPOP man's name.

The librarian went and got a tissue and

blew her nose.

And then she said, "Jack spent a lot of time here, you know. He sat in that old chair at the back almost every day. He always had his nose in a new book. Wasn't much of a talker but he loved his books. I wondered where he'd got to."

And then Mrs Bottery laughed and said, "You know, I think he must have read almost every book in here over the years. I think he was trying to read them all!"

That's when I gasped.

And Jodi's eyes went wide.

Because we'd just discovered the phantom

LOLLIPOP man's

UNFINISHED BUSINESS!

When we got back to class, Maisie was still

lying on the ground and Zach

was putting loads of

wet paper towels on

her head and Mrs Seith

was there too.

As soon as Maisie saw us she jumped up and said that she was feeling much better and Mrs Jones looked really relieved.

Then when Mrs Seith AND Miss Jones EVENTUALLY finished telling me off about my tights AND going on the run, I sat down and me and Jodi told Zach and Maisie what Mrs Bottery had said about the LOLLIPOP man and that reading every book in the library was obviously his UNFINISHED BUSINESS.

Maisie said that if we could get the LOLLIPOP man to COMMUNICATE with us then he could tell us which books he hadn't read yet and we could all use our library cards to take the books out of the library and read them to him ALOUD because phantoms might not be able to turn the pages by themselves with their GHOSTY HANDS.

Danger in The Den!

The next morning I didn't get to school until break because I had a dentist appointment. But when I got there, the new **LOLLIPOP** lady had already gone back inside the school. And even though it's only a tiny road, you're not really supposed to cross it without the new LOLLIPOP lady, or one of the teachers or one of the Year 6 Prefects.

So I started waving at everyone in the playground to try to get someone's attention and THAT'S when I heard someone say, "Time to cross, lass."

I gasped and dropped my school bag.

It was him!

THE PHANTOM LOLLIPOP MAN!

I stood there frozen to the spot, just STARING at him because this was the first time I'd seen him since he was a PHANTOM. I was just about to run all the way home when he walked out into the middle of the road and held up his LOLLIPOP stick.

Then he looked at me and said, "Across you go."

I had

what to do so I just did what the phantom LOLLIPOP man said and crossed the road.

And when I got to the other side I RAN.

When I got to The Den I BURST through the door. And that's when I saw that Jodi, Zach and Maisie were all wearing some sort of weird

GHOST BURN
PROTECTION
SUITS

made out of plastic bags and egg boxes. And there were books EVERYWHERE.

Then Zach said, "Where have you been? We've used all of our library cards to take as many books out as we could and Maisie says she'd going to read every single one to the phantom **LOLLIPOP** man if she has to."

So that's when I said, "STOP!" And everyone looked

So I quickly explained what had happened

when I was crossing the road and Jodi said,
"He must be ready to COMMUNICATE
WITH US!"

And THAT'S when someone knocked on
the door.

Everyone FROZE because we're the only
ones who know about The Den.

Jodi said that it was probably just Gary
Petrie and that he might have followed us.
So she got up and opened the door.

But it definitely WASN'T Gary Petrie.
And I knew that Jodi must have been
right about the phantom being ready to
COMMUNICATE with us.

Because it was

THE PHANTOM
LOLLIPOP MAN!!

Mr Invisible

Zach got such a fright he jumped up and tripped over the bucket he'd been sitting on and landed on the ground.

I looked at Jodi but she was sort of **FROZEN TO THE SPOT**. And she had her mouth wide open.

And that's when Maisie walked forward and said, "Hello, Jack. It's good to see you."

And the phantom LOLLIPOP man stopped frowning and did an almost-smile. And then he said, "Here. That one over there dropped this."

I watched as the LOLLIPOP man pointed at me and then handed Maisie my bag. And that's when I remembered I'd dropped it before when I got a fright.

Maisie turned and handed me my bag and I gulped and took it from her.

Then Maisie turned back to the LOLLIPOP man and said, "Would you like a cup of tea?" And Jodi sort of blinked and looked at me and I knew that she was in

SHOCK.

I was SURE that the LOLLIPOP man would say no or that he would just start to disappear in front of our eyes.

But he didn't. The LOLLIPOP man looked a bit surprised at being asked about the tea and he said, "Oh. Um. I suppose so, yes. I could use a cup of tea. I'm frozen."

Jodi moved away from the door and let the phantom LOLLIPOP man in and Zach jumped up and gave him a bucket to sit on.

Maisie asked Zach if he would please make the tea because Zach always makes the tea and Zach RAN over to where the teabags are and started making loads of noise with the cups and spoons because he was obviously panicking.

Then the LOLLIPOP man said, "Don't suppose you lot are supposed to be in here, are you?"

But before we could answer the LOLLIPOP man said, "Don't worry. I won't say a word. I know all about being places you're not supposed to be."

And we knew that the LOLLIPOP man meant that he wasn't supposed to be HERE any more and that he should have PASSED OVER into the Ghost World by now.

Jodi eventually snapped out of her SHOCK and sat down on her bucket and Zach handed the phantom LOLLIPOP man a cup of tea. The LOLLIPOP man took a sip of the tea and then spat it back into the cup. And I didn't know if that's just the way phantoms drink tea or if it was because Zach used cold water from the tap.

Maisie went into her bag and took out a biscuit and gave it to the LOLLIPOP man and he seemed to be able to eat that fine. Then when he finished the biscuit he said, "Right. Well, thanks for the tea and biscuit. I'd better be off. Shouldn't really be here. But I can't seem to stop sneaking back for an hour or two each day. Habit, I suppose."

And Maisie, "We know. But before you go, can we ask you something?"

The LOLLIPOP man looked at us all for a second and then he sighed a bit and said, "Suppose I can't stop you."

So that's when Maisie started asking him

about the library and if he still went there and if he wanted to read all the books in the library.

The **LOLLIPOP** man sighed again. And then he said, "I miss being in there, surrounded by all those books. And that chair! Well, it's the comfiest chair I've ever sat on, I'll tell you that. I'm surprised you've noticed me in there. Not often people notice me. Not the teachers or the pupils. To tell you ones the truth, I've always felt like I'm invisible in this place. Don't know why I still bother coming here. Not much else for me to do. I worked here for over fifty years, did you know that?"

And we all shook our heads because we didn't.

Then the LOLLIPOP man said, "Aye. Fifty years and not so much as a farewell party. Well, that's the people at this school for you. Mr Invisible, I am. Right, I'd better be off."

We watched as the phantom LOLLIPOP man put down his cup with his shaky ghost hand and started walking towards the door and that's when I realised that the reason he had been so grumpy all these years was because he thought no one cared about him.

And that's when Maisie said, "WAIT! Can you meet us in the library tomorrow after school? Please?"

The LOLLIPOP man looked at Maisie for a bit and then he said, "I can't do that, I'm afraid. Like I said, I'm not meant to be here."

Maisie stood up and I could see that she had tears in her eyes.

And she said, "Please, Jack. PLEASE. We just need to give you something. It'll only take a minute. And then you'll be free to leave for ever. I promise!"

The phantom LOLLIPOP man scratched his ghosty, white moustache with his hand for a minute and then he said, "Fine. I'll be there." And then he left.

As soon as the door was shut I lay down on the ground because my legs felt like JELLY and my head was SPINNING.

Zach kept saying, "Did you see his shaky hands? DID YOU?" Zach said that Jack must have had to concentrate REALLY HARD to stay VISIBLE and not turn into a

NEBULOUS CLOUD

the whole time he was in here and that that was why his hands were shaking.

Then Jodi said, "So what's the plan, Maisie? Are we going to ask Jack to tell us which books he's not read when we meet him in the library tomorrow?"

And Maisie smiled and said, "No. Not

even CLOSE."

That's when Maisie told us that she didn't think reading all the books in the library WAS the LOLLIPOP man's UNFINISHED BUSINESS. She said that she thought the LOLLIPOP man was upset because no one ever

NOTICED HIM

when he was ALIVE and that his funeral must have already passed and that no one from school even went to it to say goodbye and that that was TERRIBLE.

That's when I remembered that everyone

we spoke to in the school didn't seem to know the LOLLIPOP man very well and that some of them didn't even know his name.

Then Maisie said, "So that's why he has to meet us in the library after school tomorrow. We're going to invite all the staff and bring cake and give him the biggest goodbye party EVER!"

Phantom Party!

The next day, I was really nervous about the Phantom Party because Maisie had made us tell all the teachers that it was a "CELEBRATION OF THE LOLLIPOP MAN'S LIFE" and that we would be reading a POEM and putting up the POSTER and that there would be LOTS of cake. But she hadn't told ANYONE about the fact that the LOLLIPOP man was actually going to be there in the

PHANTOM FLESH.

Me, Jodi and Zach had spent the night before making the poster and writing the poem. And Maisie had been baking like MAD in her kitchen with her mum and she kept sending us photos of all the different cakes they had made. Then when it was half an hour before the party, Miss Jones let us leave class early so that we could go to the

library and set everything up.

Then when we got there we all

GASPED

because the librarian had made the library

look REALLY POSH with decorations and

lamps and she was wearing a long dress and

everything!

Then the dinner ladies turned up and they'd brought LOADS of sausage rolls and sandwiches and MINI SHEPHERD'S PIES!

Zach helped Maisie set up all her cakes and then Maisie wrote "WE'LL MISS YOU, JACK!" on the biggest cake with pink icing.

Me and Jodi put up the poster and it had LOADS of stuff on it that we'd found out Jack liked, like a LOLLIPOP stick, and a drawing of his favourite chair and loads of books and some biscuits.

Then the head teacher came over and handed us something in a box and said, "I hope this is OK. The office ladies told me

you were raising money for one, so the rest of the teachers and I thought we'd help you out."

And we opened it and saw that it was better than OK actually because it was a GOLD PLAQUE that you hang on the wall and it was engraved and EVERYTHING. And it said,

In Memory of Jack the Lollipop Man,

who kept us safe for 53 years.

We'll always remember you.

As soon as we showed Maisie, she burst out crying and said that they were HAPPY TEARS because it was obvious that all the teachers DID care about the LOLLIPOP man and that maybe they just hadn't been very good at showing it when he was alive.

Then all of a sudden, the end-of-day bell went and Maisie told everyone to get ready for the

BIG SURPRISE.

And THAT'S when the phantom LOLLIPOP man walked into the library.

And the thing that I was nervous about happening HAPPENED.

EVERYONE
STARTED
'SCREAMING!'

The office ladies fainted and Mrs Bottery was running around with her hands in her hair and Miss Jones sort of fell to the ground and was mumbling something and

the dinner ladies wouldn't stop screaming
and Mr Graves fainted RIGHT on top of a
SHEPHERD'S PIE! It was CHAOS!

And then Maisie shouted, "SURPRISE!!"

That's Against a LOLLIPOP Man's Human Rights!

Once the ambulance had taken some of the office ladies away, we all went over to where the LOLLIPOP man was having a seat because he looked a bit confused.

So that's when I explained to him that people are never really PREPARED to see a

PHANTOM and that it can be quite scary for them the first time they see someone who has passed away.

The LOLLIPOP man's eyes went

when I said that.

And then he said, "WHAT? I'M not DEAD!! Well, not YET anyway. But if everyone keeps on screaming it might not be long!"

Maisie STARED at the LOLLIPOP man and then she took her finger and started poking his face a bit. And then we all did it

until he said, "Enough!"

The LOLLIPOP man asked us why on earth we thought he had passed away so we told him about the new LOLLIPOP lady and how the office ladies had said he had MOVED ON and that's when he told us that

MOVED ON doesn't mean the same thing as **PASSED AWAY**. And that moved on just means you've stopped doing the thing you were doing and started doing something else.

That's when the **LOLLIPOP** man told us that he had **RETIRED** from his job. And he said that he **HATED** being retired and that even though he wasn't really allowed to, he still put on his old uniform some days and snuck into school with his old **LOLLIPOP** stick and sometimes even helped people cross the road when Mabel had gone back inside.

Then he said that he also sneaked into the library when Mrs Bottery wasn't paying attention so he could sit in his chair and read the books.

Zach asked the LOLLIPOP man why he didn't like being retired and he said that there wasn't really anything for him to do at home since his wife passed away. And then he went quiet for a bit.

Then the LOLLIPOP man said, "I didn't want to retire, you know. But the council sent me a letter saying I'm too old to keep working here."

I got REALLY annoyed when the

LOLLIPOP man said that, because it isn't very nice of the council people to send you a letter telling you that you are too old to do stuff.

And then Jodi said that we should write a letter back to them about the LOLLIPOP man's

HUMAN RIGHTS.

And we all agreed that we definitely should. That made the LOLLIPOP man do his ALMOST-SMILE and then he asked us if we had really thought that he was a phantom and we said yes and that made him smile a proper smile.

Jodi told the LOLLIPOP man about the

NEBULOUS CLOUD

and the strange SMOKY SMELL behind the old bike shed. And the LOLLIPOP man said, "SHHHHHH! Don't be letting people hear you say that! That's where I smoke my pipe!"

And we realised that the smoke we saw had been coming from the LOLLIPOP man's pipe and that he must have hidden around the corner when he heard us coming. And Jodi said, "Well, if it wasn't your ghost cloud that set off the fire alarm, what was it? You didn't smoke your pipe INSIDE the school, did you?!"

But the LOLLIPOP man said that he definitely DIDN'T and that he'd actually been NAPPING in his library chair when the fire alarm went off and that he'd had to DUCK DOWN when he was going past the windows and sneak out the front entrance so no one found out he'd been coming back into the school after he retired. And that made me giggle because it DEFINITELY

explained the

Then a voice said, "It was me."

And we turned around and saw Gary Petrie and he was eating a HUGE bit of cake (even though we hadn't actually CUT any of the cakes yet!).

I hadn't even REALISED Gary Petrie was invited to the Phantom Party but then Maisie said that she'd invited him because he'd helped the investigation.

That's when Gary Petrie said that HE set

the fire alarm off because he'd heard us say that we saw SMOKE and that that's what you're meant to do when you see smoke and suspect a FIRE.

Then Gary said, "MAYBE if you'd told me ALL THE FACTS then I wouldn't have set the fire alarm off. And I wouldn't have had to follow you all the time and listen outside your DEN."

And we all GASPED when Gary said that because he knew about THE DEN!

Then Jodi said, "YOU caused the BLACKOUT, didn't you?"

And even though Gary Petrie wouldn't

admit it we all KNEW that it had been him because he was trying not to laugh and also because we remembered that the light switch is on the outside of The Den.

Maisie sent Gary away (because Jodi was looking REALLY MAD!) and he went because Maisie said he could have more cake.

And that's when we told the LOLLIPOP man about the

and how we'd smelled a weird, orange-y smell next to his library chair and that phantoms have UNEXPLAINED SMELLS.

And the LOLLIPOP man laughed and said, "Follow me."

So we did. And he took us over to his chair and pointed to the wall and that's when we saw the AIR FRESHENER. Then he said, "It's one of those ones that are set to spray every so often. Makes a really annoying whooshing sound. Drives me nuts. And my wife used to wonder why I came home smelling of perfume!"

And when the LOLLIPOP man said that, it made me a bit sad because I knew that when he went home smelling of perfume now there wasn't anyone there to smell it.

That's when Maisie grabbed the LOLLIPOP man and gave him a great big hug and started jumping up and down, yelling,

"HE'S ALIVE! JACK'S ALIIIIIIIIIIIIIIIIIVE!"

Then everyone started coming up to the LOLLIPOP man and giving him really long hugs and loads of people were crying and the LOLLIPOP man looked really surprised about all the hugs and stuff and we knew that it was because he thought he had practically been INVISIBLE to everyone for fifty years.

Then Jodi took the LOLLIPOP man over to see his poster and Maisie showed him his cake and I got up on one of the chairs and read out the poem we wrote for Jack when we thought he had passed away.

Everyone said that I did a GREAT job and I think I did because it is not easy to take out words like PHANTOM and DEAD and FUNERAL and put other words in instead when you only have two minutes to fix it.

The LOLLIPOP man cut his cake and everyone cheered and thanked him for working at our school and shook his hand and wished him a happy retirement.

And when Maisie showed him the wall plaque the LOLLIPOP man nodded and pretended he was just rubbing his eye but we all knew he was crying a bit with happiness. Then Mrs Bottery said that we should put it up in the library, above Jack's Chair (which is what she calls it now), and that made the LOLLIPOP man smile.

Once the party was finished, we walked the LOLLIPOP man out and that's when he said, "Thank you, by the way, for all that in there. You're a good bunch, you are."

And we all said that he was welcome and Maisie made us stand and watch the LOLLIPOP man walking away until we couldn't see him any more.

And then I said, "Let's go. We've got work to do!"

Ziggy & Jack

A few weeks later, we all got a **BIG SURPRISE** because when we were leaving school the **LOLLIPOP** man was waiting for us at the school gates and he had a **DOG** with him!

We all ran over and Maisie gave him a hug

and we asked loads of questions about the dog.

That's when the LOLLIPOP man said, "This is Ziggy. I thought you might like to meet him. It was a bit too quiet in the house so I thought I'd get someone to keep me company."

And then the LOLLIPOP man looked at Ziggy and said, "It's not quiet at ALL any more, is it? You've a fair set of lungs on you, haven't you?"

Ziggy looked up at the LOLLIPOP man and barked and we all laughed and petted Ziggy for ages.

Then Zach lay on the ground and Ziggy walked all over him and licked his face and it was HILARIOUS.

Then the LOLLIPOP man said, "I also thought you lot might have something to do with this here. Would that be right?"

Then he reached into his pocket and

took out a piece of paper and gave it to us. And it was a letter from THE COUNCIL and along the top it said:

VOLUNTEER LIBRARY ASSISTANT – ST VINCENT'S PRIMARY SCHOOL

We were all MEGA HAPPY because we knew that the letter Mrs Bottery had helped us write and send to the council had WORKED!!

Maisie said, "Are you going to take the job? Are you coming back?!"

And the LOLLIPOP man said that he

WAS. But only for an hour or two in the mornings so he could get back to give Ziggy his lunch and take him for his afternoon walk.

Then he said, "Someone's got to make sure that gold plaque gets polished every day, haven't they?"

That's when we all started jumping up and down and yelling,

☆ — "JACK'S BACK! — ☆
☆ JACK'S BACK!" ☆

And Ziggy started howling along with us and he wouldn't stop until we stopped.

And as soon as we started cheering again Ziggy started howling again too!

And the LOLLIPOP man just shook his head at us and did his almost-smile.

Acknowledgements

I'd like to say a huge thank you to all the amazing school support staff who contribute so much to their schools and the experiences of the pupils. Schools just wouldn't work without you.

Thanks also to Thomas for the brilliant illustrations — I love them!

And a huge thanks to my superhero editor, Kirsty. The Izzy books wouldn't be the same without you. (Please never leave me!!)

And, as always, love and thanks to Andy for all your support (and take-aways).